DOBBY
AND BUCKBEAK

A Division of Insight Editions, LP
San Rafael, California

Harry Potter

DOBBY

A Behind-the-Scenes Look at House-Elves of the Harry Potter Films

By Jody Revenson

INTRODUCTION

A house-elf is required to serve one wizarding family for his or her entire life, and house-elves are very faithful to their masters. Any command their master gives them must be obeyed, though it helps to be specific, as a house-elf may not perform the order exactly as it was meant to be done! When house-elves don't follow instructions, or say something bad about their master, they are forced to punish themselves. Although house-elves are small, they can actually do incredibly powerful magic—and without the use of a wand! Since house-elves can only be released from their slavery by a gift from their master of a piece of clothing, they often wear a filthy discarded tea towel or pillowcase.

A WELL-LOVED CHARACTER

Dobby's first appearance in the Harry Potter movies was in *Harry Potter and the Chamber of Secrets*, when the house-elf is discovered in Harry's bedroom at the Dursleys'. Dobby is trying to keep Harry from going back to Hogwarts, where he may be harmed. Dobby was already a big favorite of readers of the books, so it was important that when he was brought to life on-screen, he would be just as beloved.

DOBBY DECISIONS

The director of *Harry Potter and the Chamber of Secrets*, Chris Columbus, wanted to make sure that Dobby would feel very real. At first, the filmmakers thought that Dobby could be a puppet that would be operated on set, making it easier for the actors to interact with him. But it was soon decided that Dobby would become the film series' first fully computer-generated major character.

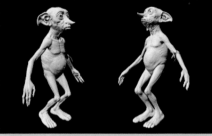

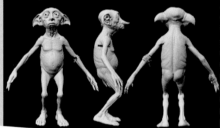

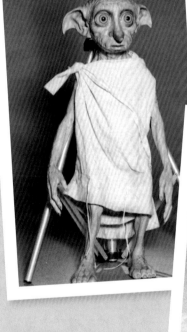

LOOK HERE!

As Dobby wouldn't physically interact with Harry Potter or other characters on the film set, the filmmakers used a tennis ball on a stick in his place. This is a long-used method that allows actors to focus on where the character should be. It also provides the computer animators with a visual reference for where to place the character within the scene.

EYES ON THE BALL

Chris Columbus, director of *Chamber of Secrets*, knew that it would be a challenge to direct Daniel Radcliffe's (Harry Potter) scenes when he interacts with Dobby. "He wouldn't have anyone in the room to act with," says Chris. "He was basically acting with a little green tennis ball! But Dan was so focused he made you believe that Dobby was there."

CREATING DOBBY'S LOOK

CGI, which stands for "computer-generated imagery," involves many steps between coming up with the design of the character and putting that character on-screen. The process for Dobby started with ideas for what the house-elf would look like, which were drawn by visual development artists. Dobby went through many design ideas before the big-eyed, bat-eared, pointy-nosed house-elf emerged. The artists also thought about Dobby's background as a servant to the Malfoy family, and so he was given a gray, pale "prisoner of war" appearance, with grimy skin and little or no muscles.

"Master has given Dobby a sock! Master has presented Dobby with clothes! Dobby is free!"

—DOBBY, *HARRY POTTER AND THE CHAMBER OF SECRETS* FILM

A MODEL HOUSE-ELF

Once Dobby's look was established, the creature shop, headed by Nick Dudman, created a full-size three-dimensional model made of silicone. The model had a metal skeleton inside so that its joints could be placed into any position. And then they made a few more models of Dobby in exactly the same way. Each model was fully painted, with lots and lots of details, right down to the veins in his eyes and the wrinkles on his skin. "Dobby's pasty and pale and covered with dirt and dressed in a rag," says Nick. "It may be an awful lot of work that needed to be done, but I think Dobby is a bit more real because we went through this process."

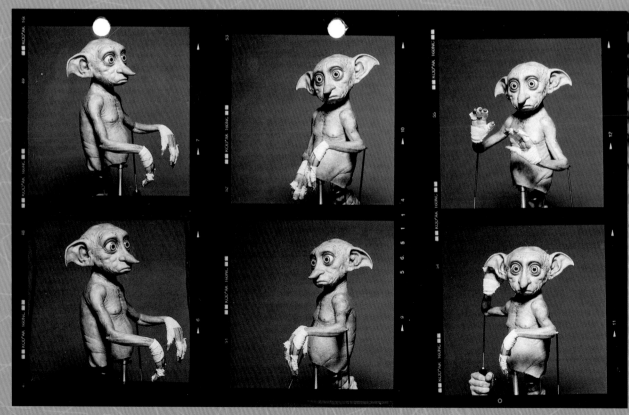

The life-size model of Dobby with the completely functioning armature inside was occasionally posed on the set before a scene was filmed. This helped the actors to know the specific place to look where Dobby would be, and for the lighting designers to make sure that Dobby's lighting would be correct on the set. Then the model would be taken away, and the scene would be filmed with just the human actors. Dobby would be placed back into the scene by the animation team.

MODEL HOME

One of the life-size Dobby models used in the filming of *Harry Potter and the Chamber of Secrets* sits in the office of director Chris Columbus. "He guards the office for me," says Chris. "We did use the model for some over-the-shoulder shots in the movie. But Dobby was always going to be a CGI character, and I'm very proud of how he turned out." Another one of the Dobby models was given to author J.K. Rowling, who gifted it to a building in Aberdeen, Scotland, that became a movie theater.

FACIAL EXPRESSIONS

Dobby's movement for *Harry Potter and the Chamber of Secrets* was achieved completely within the computer. However, actor Toby Jones, who performed the voice of the house-elf, would first act out Dobby's scenes for the animators. His facial expressions and physical movements would inspire the digital performance created by the computer effects team. The animators did add one facial expression of their own, though: Dobby's smile always turns up on the left side of his mouth whether or not he is facing that way on-screen.

PROPS TO THE CGI TEAM

When Dobby tries to punish himself in *Harry Potter and the Chamber of Secrets* by banging his head with a lamp in Harry's bedroom, the scene was originally filmed with the real props needed on Harry's desk: a pencil cup, a photo album, a glass of water, and a lamp. But then the filmmakers realized that Dobby was the one who was actually interacting with the props. So the special effects team erased the originals in the film and replaced them with computer-animated versions.

VERY SPECIAL EFFECTS

In addition to Dobby and the props used in Harry's bedroom in *Chamber of Secrets*, the special effects team also needed to create his shadow on the walls as he bounced around the room and the tears on his face when he cried.

PIECE OF CAKE

It was a computer-generated cake that floated across the room when Dobby snapped his fingers to send it in the direction of the Dursleys' guests at the beginning of *Harry Potter and the Chamber of Secrets*, but it was a real cake with whipped cream and sugared violets that fell onto Mrs. Mason's head!

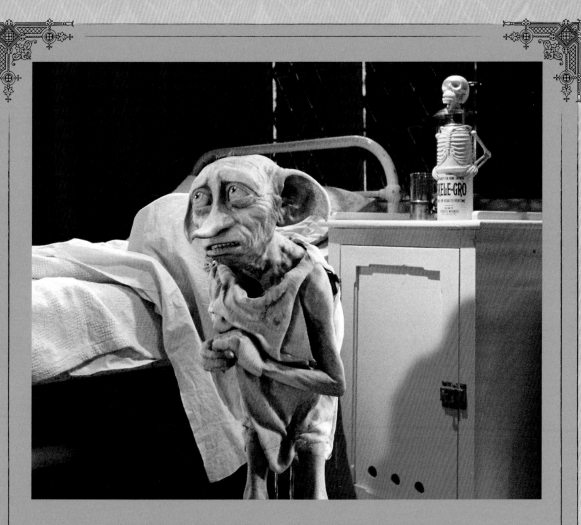

A MOVING HOUSE-ELF

For *Harry Potter and the Chamber of Secrets*, the computer animation team wanted to make sure that Dobby always stood or moved like a house-elf who had been treated badly by his wizarding family for years. Very often, Dobby would wrap his arms around himself or curl inward so he could protect his body and be a smaller target. After Dobby is freed, his posture changes, and he walks much taller and straighter.

Lucius Malfoy and Dobby

For Jason Isaacs, who played Lucius Malfoy in the Harry Potter films, acting alongside Dobby was a lesson of learning to believe in the unseen. "The first time I worked with Dobby," he says, "I asked, 'So where is Dobby going to be in the room? Where should I look?' And I was told, 'Well, wherever you look, that's where we'll put him!'"

"Dobby is used to death threats, sir. Dobby gets them five times a day at home."

—DOBBY, HARRY POTTER AND THE CHAMBER OF SECRETS FILM

A LOST HOUSE-ELF

Winky is a female house-elf in the book
Harry Potter and the Goblet of Fire who
Harry meets at the Quidditch World
Cup. The visual development artists
illustrated ideas of what she would look
like, but unfortunately the character did
not make it into the movie.

KREACHER

Kreacher, who we first meet in *Harry Potter and the Order of the Phoenix*, is the house-elf for the Black family, but he despises his current master, Sirius Black. Where Dobby is very likable and energetic, Kreacher is the complete opposite. Kreacher moves slowly, acts slowly, and does both with a noticeable grumble.

TOUJOURS ✶ PUR ✶

AN AWFUL HOUSE ELF

"Yes, he's awful," laughs Nick Dudman, head of the creature shop. "He's the Black family's aged, crumbly retainer. And he hates everybody who isn't a pureblood wizard—his loyalties are very much on the dark side." Nick wanted to make the nasty house-elf as revolting and ghastly in every way possible. "His ears droop much, much more than Dobby's, he's flappy all over, he's bent over with age, and he barely moves when he walks."

AN UNMOVING HOUSE-ELF

The animators who work on a film usually create CGI characters that can fly, like Buckbeak the Hippogriff in *Harry Potter and the Prisoner of Azkaban*, or swim like the Grindylows in *Harry Potter and the Goblet of Fire*. So to create Kreacher they had to go against their usual instincts in order to bring the elderly, bile-spewing house-elf to life. They created a performance with very little movement, deciding that at Kreacher's age, the character would, of course, walk slowly. Kreacher almost skulks, and always seems to be creeping up on people, which makes him all the more unappealing.

KREACHER'S VOICE

Kreacher was voiced by Timothy Bateson for *Order of the Phoenix*, then Simon McBurney for *Harry Potter and the Deathly Hallows – Part 1*. Just like Toby Jones for Dobby, these actors' voice performances were filmed, but it was up to the animators to create the old house-elf's plodding movements and facial expressions.

EARS TO YOU

The designers had fun creating Kreacher's aged, collapsing skin, which was appropriately soft and stretchy for such an elderly character. They also gave him long, dragging ears that were complete with ear hair, and a little hair on his head, unlike Dobby. Kreacher was given a noticeable hunchbacked posture, a dewlap under his chin, watery eyes, and a stooped stance that really portrayed disgust and intolerance.

BEHIND THE CURTAIN

Kreacher is seen cleaning and talking to a muttering curtain-covered portrait in the hallway of number twelve, Grimmauld Place in *Harry Potter and the Order of the Phoenix*. The painting is that of Sirius's mother, Walburga.

"Nasty brat standing there as bold as brass. Harry Potter, the boy who stopped the Dark Lord. Friend of Mudbloods and blood-traitors alike. If my poor mistress only knew . . ."
—KREACHER, *HARRY POTTER AND THE ORDER OF THE PHOENIX* FILM

PERFORMANCE ARTIST

Actor Timothy Bateson, Kreacher's voice in *Harry Potter and the Order of the Phoenix*, was filmed as he sat in a chair and read his lines, and the team used his facial expressions and mannerisms as performance reference. But the actual combination of body language, attitude, how Kreacher moved around, and how he reacted to Harry was entirely the creation of the animation team, who were proud that Kreacher was thought of as no less than a living being.

THE HOUSE-ELVES OF GRIMMAULD PLACE

In *Harry Potter and the Order of the Phoenix*, Harry observes a curious practice during his first visit to number twelve, Grimmauld Place, Sirius Black's family home and the headquarters of the Order of the Phoenix. Placed around the staircase to the second floor, the heads of the former house-elves for the Black family are preserved and displayed in tall glass bell jars.

HEAD DESIGNER

Each ancient house-elf in the Black house had distinctive hair, teeth, and snouts. Unlike the bald Dobby and the nearly bald Kreacher, these house-elves were given unique hairstyles. Rob Bliss, the visual development artist, also explored different hats and collars for the house-elves, which help indicate the time period they served the family.

HOUSE-ELF ARMOR

When writing a movie, the filmmakers explore many ideas, but not all of them make it to the final film. For *Harry Potter and the Half-Blood Prince*, it was proposed that armored house-elf statues in the entrance hall stairway of Hogwarts would come to life by digital animation. Although the visual development artists put these ideas on paper, they didn't make it into the movie.

CO-CREATURES

In *Harry Potter and the Deathly Hallows – Part 1*, Harry, Ron, and Hermione hide out at number twelve, Grimmauld Place. There they meet up with both house-elves, Dobby and Kreacher. Even though the actors who voiced them would not be seen in the film, they acted out the entire scene on the set so the animators could catch the way they looked at each other and their physical interactions. Then the scene was done again with actors of short stature playing the roles. This helped the other actors as they no longer had to look at a tennis ball! The actors playing Dobby and Kreacher were covered in gray outfits that had reference points placed on them to help the animators with keeping their positions during the scene. Then the computer artists used all these performances as reference for creating the house-elves.

OLD FRIENDS

For their last appearances in the film series, in *Harry Potter and the Deathly Hallows – Part 1*, the director and visual effects team felt that the audience needed to have more of an emotional connection with Dobby, and even Kreacher. They were "humanized," in that their features were softened and, as several years had passed, they were made to look older.

"*Dobby has no master! Dobby is a free elf, and Dobby has come to save Harry Potter and his friends!*"
—DOBBY, HARRY POTTER AND THE DEATHLY HALLOWS – PART 1

MAKEOVERS

For *Harry Potter and the Deathly Hallows – Part 1*, Dobby's arms were shortened, his neck and face were smoothed out, and his eyes were reshaped to appear less saucerlike and less bulging. He is still dressed in a tea towel, but it's much cleaner, and he's wearing shoes. He also had a softer, more radiant look, which the filmmakers felt would make him even more sympathetic.

Kreacher also had a makeover for *Deathly Hallows – Part 1*, making his skin smoother as well, and reducing the size of his nose. They also trimmed his ear hair.

A BEAUTIFUL PASSING

The only time a full Dobby model was used for filming was in *Harry Potter and the Deathly Hallows – Part 1*, when Harry holds the dying Dobby in his arms. Dobby's death on the beach at Shell Cottage involved not only the life-size model and the CGI version of the character but also a real-life body double who performed in the scene. This was not Toby Jones, however, as he's much taller, so they used a person of short stature. When Dobby passes away, the visual effects designers made his eyes appear watery and slowly changed the texture of his skin to make him appear paler and paler.

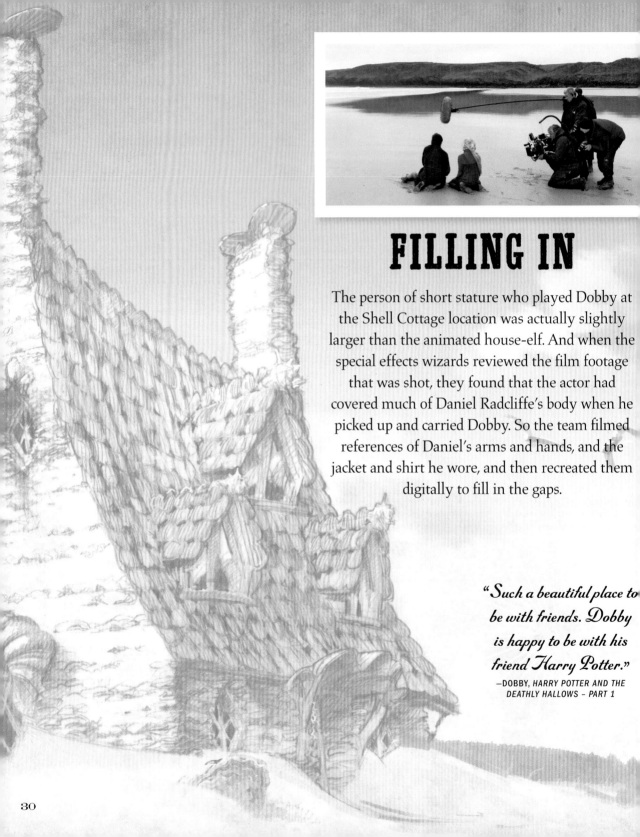

FILLING IN

The person of short stature who played Dobby at the Shell Cottage location was actually slightly larger than the animated house-elf. And when the special effects wizards reviewed the film footage that was shot, they found that the actor had covered much of Daniel Radcliffe's body when he picked up and carried Dobby. So the team filmed references of Daniel's arms and hands, and the jacket and shirt he wore, and then recreated them digitally to fill in the gaps.

"Such a beautiful place to be with friends. Dobby is happy to be with his friend Harry Potter."
—DOBBY, HARRY POTTER AND THE DEATHLY HALLOWS – PART 1

A PERFECT END

The death of Dobby is a very strong, emotional scene, and the filmmakers thought that this was the best way to end the movie. "After several ideas, we realized that we should end it with the burial of Dobby," says director David Yates, "which enforces Harry's commitment to carry on and find the means with which to defeat the Dark Lord, no matter what." To emphasize Harry's strong connection to Dobby, Harry chooses to bury him properly by hand, without the use of magic. Actor Daniel Radcliffe thought it was fitting and right. "Harry wants to invest as much love in Dobby's burial as Dobby showed him throughout his life," he explains.

HERE LIES DOBBY A FREE ELF

MAKE IT YOUR OWN

One of the great things about IncrediBuilds models is that each one is completely customizable. The untreated natural wood can be decorated with paints, pencils, pens, beads, sequins—the list goes on and on!

Before you start building and decorating your model, though, read through the included instruction sheet so you understand how all the pieces come together. Then, choose a theme and make a plan. Do you want to make an exact replica of Dobby or something completely different? Why not try matching Dobby's pillowcase to the colors of your favorite Hogwarts house? The choice is yours! Here is an example to get those creative juices flowing.

TIPS BEFORE YOU BEGIN

*As a general rule of thumb, you'll want to use pens and pencils *before* building the model and paints *after* building the model.

*When making a replica, it's always good to study an actual image of what you are trying to copy. Look closely at details and brainstorm how you can recreate them.

PAINTING DOBBY

1. For Dobby, it is very helpful to paint certain pieces before fully assembling the model. To start, paint the assembled head piece just after step 7 in the instructions. Choose a main color that comes close to matching the house-elf's skin color. Then after applying a base coat of that color, fill in the details of his face, such as the eyes.

2. Next, using the same base color you did for Dobby's face, paint both arms. Make sure to leave the tab at the shoulder blank. This will make it easier to attach the arms to the body.

3. **Continue building to step 18.** Now paint Dobby's pillowcase. A neutral color was used here to reflect Dobby's actual clothes in the film.

4. **Next, paint the legs after step 20.** After Dobby is completely assembled, you can add more details.

5. Using a rough dry brush, dab the pillowcase with a darker color. You don't need much paint to give the pillowcase a worn-out look. Experiment with it. If you don't like the effect, you can always paint over it!

6. For Dobby's body, paint a few small gray lines. Smudge the lines with your finger or brush to complete Dobby's hard-working look.

Harry Potter

BUCKBEAK

A Behind-the-Scenes Look at Everyone's Favorite Hippogriff

By Jody Revenson

INTRODUCTION

In *Harry Potter and the Prisoner of Azkaban*, the first fantastic beast presented by the new Care of Magical Creatures professor for third years, Rubeus Hagrid, is a gray-and-white Hippogriff named Buckbeak. Hippogriffs are very proud creatures, Hagrid advises, and proper etiquette must be observed when meeting one (or there might be disastrous consequences). When Hagrid asks for a student to help him with the lesson, Harry Potter unknowingly volunteers when all the other members of his class back away from the offer. The professor instructs Harry to bow to the Hippogriff first, then wait to see if the creature bows back. If Buckbeak does bow, Harry can touch him. Fortunately, Buckbeak responds favorably to the salutation and not only lets Harry stroke him but also takes the student for a memorable flight. Later on, Buckbeak is very important in the rescue of Sirius Black.

"First thing you want to know about Hippogriffs is that they're very proud creatures. Very easily offended. You don't want to insult a Hippogriff. It may just be the last thing you ever do. Now—who'd like to come and say hello?"

—Rubeus Hagrid, *Harry Potter and the Prisoner of Azkaban*

A Very Mixed-Up Creature

"The Hippogriff is a kind of half-horse, half-eagle creature. Hagrid is obsessed with having pretty much lethal creatures as pets!"

—Daniel Radcliffe (Harry Potter), *Harry Potter and the Prisoner of Azkaban: Ultimate Edition*, "Creating the World of Harry Potter, Part 3: Creatures"

Hippogriffs are creatures with a long mythological history. The word *Hippogriff* comes from the Greek word *hippos*, which was their word for horse, and an Old French word, *grifo*, which came from the Latin word for griffin, *gryphus*. A Hippogriff is the offspring of a horse and a griffin, which itself is the offspring of an eagle and a lion. The designers of Buckbeak looked at legendary depictions of the creature and consulted with veterinarians so that there would be an anatomical logic to Buckbeak's shape and movement. They also visited bird sanctuaries to observe birds in flight and studied horses walking and galloping in fields outside of London.

We Can Do That!

For any film with fantasy elements, lots of discussion goes on about what will be a physical effect and what will be computer-generated. The filmmakers on the Harry Potter movies always felt it was better to have a "real" creature to interact with the actors. "In our initial meetings about Buckbeak," says creature effects supervisor Nick Dudman, "we talked about having the Hippogriff sitting down in the pumpkin patch. So I said, 'We can do that.' And they said that it would be attached to a chain, and the kids would tug on that. And I said that we could do that, too. And then they said that Buckbeak would get up and walk away with them. And I said, 'Ah, no. I don't think we can do that!'"

HORSING AROUND

An early idea for how to construct Buckbeak was to build it around a horse, but Nick Dudman quickly recognized the difficulty of that choice. "The way Buckbeak's head—that of a bird—was designed, you couldn't fit a horse's head into it, and how would the animal perform, anyway?" The possibility of creating just the bird front of Buckbeak in a mechanical form was suggested, but that still meant that when the entire creature was seen, it would need to be computer-generated. Eventually, it was decided that Buckbeak would be a mixture of digital and physical versions, as it was actually more economical to use full-size creatures for several scenes.

Buckbeak Times Four

"Isn't he beautiful?
Say hello to Buckbeak."

—Rubeus Hagrid, *Harry Potter and the Prisoner of Azkaban*

Four variations of Buckbeak were created for *Harry Potter and the Prisoner of Azkaban* to fulfill different purposes and uses. "We had a lying-down Hippogriff that was built for the pumpkin patch," explains creature efffects supervisor Nick Dudman. "Then we had a standing Hippogriff set on a counterbalanced pole arm for foreground shots." This pole arm worked the same way a seesaw does, with a weight at the end opposite Buckbeak so that its operators could control the creature's movements. "The third was a freestanding background Hippogriff that didn't have operators attached to it, so we didn't have to use digital technology to remove them from the shot." The fourth Buckbeak was computer-generated and was used whenever Buckbeak flew or walked.

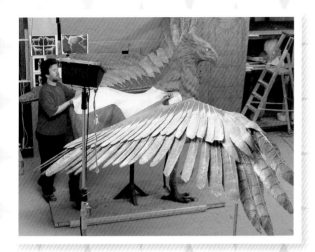

A PLAYFUL PERSONALITY

In addition to Buckbeak's physical mechanics, the animators also needed to consider what his personality would be and how it would be shown. "We did a lot of tests before we started working on the movie," says visual effects supervisor Roger Guyett. "For Buckbeak, we asked ourselves, what kind of animal is he—is he excitable? Is he sad? And how do you show that in a shot?" Early animation of Buckbeak had him jumping around in a very playful manner, acting very much like a puppy. But director Alfonso Cuarón wanted the visual effects team to "age" him up, saying that Buckbeak should be more like a "sloppy teenager." Cuarón also asked that Buckbeak be "a mixture of regal elegance when he is flying and clumsiness back on land."

A Creature of Character

"The Hippogriff scared me," says screenwriter Steve Kloves. "I mean, how are you going to bring this creature to the screen?" Director Alfonso Cuarón felt that every scene should be character-defining. "These different creatures are different extensions of the characters," says Cuarón. "The Hippogriff is one extension of Harry's coming-of-age when he discovers his inner power and his freedom." Cuarón felt that the thirteen-year-old Harry was realizing a new power he has to learn to control, and he has to learn to surrender to it in order to fly. "And once he's up in the air and extends his arms," Kloves continues, "he's no longer burdened by all the problems he has when he's on the ground. If he could only fly forever, he'd be all right."

47

Learning to Walk

One of the most important challenges in creating an original creature for the movies is to make sure they can actually do what they're supposed to do. Computers have helped this process out immeasurably. "We can understand the anatomy of a Hippogriff only up to a certain point," says creature effects supervisor Nick Dudman. "So first we create a fully realized model—a three-dimensional sculpt called a maquette—which is cyber-scanned into the computer. And, with that, the visual effects team can make the creature fly—and more important, land. Then they'll come back to us and say, 'You do realize that he'd trip over his own knees or fall to the ground when he's carrying passengers, don't you?' They'll explain that by lengthening his spine six inches, these problems would be solved." Nick appreciated these early CG studies as a very useful step in creating a realistic creature.

FIRST IMPRESSIONS

"**B**uckbeak was one of the most complicated elements because he was so interactive with our characters," says director Alfonso Cuarón. "That was a big challenge in terms of visual effects." The animators needed to express Buckbeak's character and his relationship to Harry Potter in the short time he is initially on screen. "Buckbeak doesn't talk," explains animation supervisor Michael Eames, "and he has a beak, with all the lack of expression implicit in that. So you look for everything that can help you convey what you want. One way was to use cues from the actors. For example, when Harry and Buckbeak first meet, we used a slight slip in Harry's posture and bounced that off Buckbeak as its reaction."

Eagle Eyes

"Now, have to let him make the first move. It's only polite. So, step up, give him a nice bow, then you wait to see if he bows back. If he does, you can go and touch him. If not . . . well, we'll get to that later."

—Rubeus Hagrid, *Harry Potter and the Prisoner of Azkaban*

Buckbeak's bird half was based on that of a golden eagle. Then visual development artists tested several color choices for his feathers, landing on combinations of gray and white. The Hippogriff's construction was supervised by key animatronic model designer Valerie "Val" Jones-Mendosa. "Buckbeak was one of the most challenging creatures I've ever worked on," she says. "We worked closely with mechanical engineers to replicate the exact wing movement and skeleton of a real bird. It took a team of twenty to build three versions of him." The animatronic model created for Harry Potter's introduction to Buckbeak could bow and move two of its legs. The Hippogriff in the pumpkin patch was able to move its wings, neck, eyes, tongue, and beak. Buckbeak's plaintive "caw" was that of a limpkin, provided by Macaulay Library at Cornell University's Lab of Ornithology.

BIRDS AND HORSES OF A FEATHER FLOCK TOGETHER

To create the pelt on the horse end of Buckbeak, the three maquettes were "flocked." Flocking is a very labor-intensive process that involves a team of workers. First, the area to be flocked is wetted down with a special glue, and then an electrical charge is run through it. The team then fires hairs that are oppositely charged at an area. This causes the hairs to stick and stand on end. Then the hairs are combed into their desired direction before the glue dries, which has to be done within forty minutes. If this wasn't finished within the designated time period, the team would have to start again from scratch. It took a lot of rehearsing to ensure that the correct mixes of hair colors and lengths adhered to their assigned areas. Once the flocking was finished, longer hairs were punched into the models one at a time and airbrushed artwork was added.

Featherology 101

"Think he might let yeh ride him now! . . . Over here, just behind the wing joint. Don't pull out any of his feathers 'cause he won't thank yeh for that."

—Rubeus Hagrid, *Harry Potter and the Prisoner of Azkaban*

Flocking the horse half of Buckbeak was "quite a business," says creature effects supervisor Nick Dudman, "but it was nothing compared to the front half." Each version of Buckbeak required thousands of feathers to be sorted by size and then hand-dyed and airbrushed to match a specific color scheme. Chicken and goose feathers were used, though "the biggest ones at the ends of the wings needed to be fabricated" and were molded in plastic, explains Nick. Then all the feathers were glued into place one by one onto a stretchy, tailored netting that covered the models. And remember: All three Hippogriffs had to match *exactly*. Even though Nick and Val Jones-Mendosa had worked out a timeframe for the feathering, their team was still adding feathers up to the moment Buckbeak was needed on set.

Winging It

There are definite biological rules about how birds can fly that factor into their weight and wingspan. "So, obviously, to fly something the scale of a seven-foot tall horse," says visual effects supervisor Roger Guyett, "you need really big wings!" The Hippogriff's designers worked out that the wingspan length that would allow Buckbeak to fly would be twenty-eight feet. Except that wings that size would drag on the ground when he walked and possibly even trip the Hippogriff. So, "essentially we cheated," confesses visual effects supervisor Tim Burke. "We had smaller wings when he was on the ground and bigger wings when he was flying. But hopefully you won't notice."

Featherology 102

Buckbeak's animators had as formidable a task as the creature effects team when it came to feathering the creature. As the Hippogriff is seen in full daylight and close up, the feathers needed to be as realistic as digitally possible, something that up to this point had been a challenge to computer artists. In order to achieve this, the team created the individual types of feathers to as fine a detail as possible and then designed a computer program that would move the feathers together in the same way as a real bird's. Additionally, Buckbeak's wings needed to go from wrapped against his body to extended while flying and vice versa. "We had to develop a wing that could move from fully outstretched to fully folded without interruption," says CG supervisor David Lomax. "The grooming and packing of the feathers had to be precisely correct." And they needed to achieve all this without revealing that Buckbeak had different wing lengths to perform these two actions.

Year OF THE HIPPOGRIFF

It took about a year to create Buckbeak, from drawing the initial concepts to filming the Hippogriff's scenes with Daniel Radcliffe, Robbie Coltrane, and the other actors. Creature effects supervisor Nick Dudman recalls that the design phase began in June 2002. "You have a period of time where you conceptualize the creature," says Nick, "for which the art department produced many preliminary drawings. That's narrowed down, and then you progress to the maquettes, which you can show the filmmakers. They can walk around it and ask questions about its size and movements." Maquettes of the Hippogriff were created in November, and final approvals came in January. "The creature went on set in May 2003, so you're looking at nearly a year of involvement," Nick explains. The digital decisions and creation of Buckbeak happened simultaneously, but the manufacturing period of the physical creature took four and a half months of solid work.

Beak on a Stick

In addition to the three life-size models, various other filming techniques were used during the interactions between Buckbeak and the actors. When Harry Potter (Daniel Radcliffe) is allowed to stroke the Hippogriff after their bows to each other, and, after he returns from their flight, he was actually stroking a beak on the end of a stick! This ensured that when Daniel touched the beak, we would see the correct curvature of his hand for the action. Stroking something in empty air would not have given it this realism. The beak puppet was removed digitally, and the full CGI Buckbeak was then added in.

DOING WHAT COMES NATURALLY

*"Come on, Buckbeak . . . Come and get
the nice dead ferret . . ."*

—Hermione Granger, *Harry Potter and the Prisoner of Azkaban*

The filmmakers went to great lengths to ensure that Buckbeak was as realistic as a fantastical creature could be. "It's so realistic," director Alfonso Cuarón says, "that if people watch carefully, in the scene where Buckbeak is in the paddock, you will see he actually poos. Buckbeak poos!" Cuarón came up with the idea when the team was observing the movement of horses for reference: "I saw that the horses would be very casually, very naturally, pooing. So it's not a big deal; it's just a matter-of-fact thing that Buckbeak does."

A Light Horse

There were several occasions when a real horse would stand in for Buckbeak during rehearsals so that the visual effects crew could observe how the light through the trees would shade the creature and how the shadow of the creature itself would be cast on the environment. This lighting was re-created exactly in the computer. The digital team looked for all ways possible to lend authenticity to their creations, which constantly impressed the filmmakers. "When you see Buckbeak in the movie," says executive producer Mark Radcliffe (no relation to Daniel), "and he's placed in the live-action scene, matching the light of the set with how the light falls onto the Hippogriff and the shadow movement in relation to the other actors—it is seamless."

Taking Flight

Once Harry and Buckbeak are introduced, Hagrid places the student on his back for a test flight. Daniel Radcliffe (Harry Potter) shot the sequence in a blue-screened room in a way similar to filming broom flight. But instead of hanging from wires, Daniel sat on a full-size model of just the Hippogriff's trunk that was attached to a rig arm, which was also covered in blue-screen material. The rig would reproduce preprogrammed movements provided by the animation team and was filmed by a camera that was also synced to the action. Visual effects then "composited" a filmed background of the Hogwarts grounds, the CG Hippogriff, and the footage of Daniel to create a seamless scene. They even added clouds of digital dirt that fall from Buckbeak's hooves when he takes off and lands!

On Location

T he "sitting-down" version of Buckbeak in Hagrid's pumpkin patch was constructed in England and brought to Glencoe, Scotland. Typically, an operator would be placed in a close proximity, but the Hippogriff would be sitting atop a granite hillside, so creature effects supervisor Nick Dudman knew it couldn't be operated from underneath: "We could radio-control it, but then you have to deal with great thumping motors. Where do they go? How do we deal with the sound?" Nick decided to use a variation of hydraulics called *aquatronics* for Buckbeak's big movements. This system uses cables pumped through with water instead of the oil used in hydraulics and creates smoother, more graceful shifts that can give the creature more elegance and gravity. The crew needed to be graceful, too, and not tread on the cables and damage them. Any noticeable cables were digitally erased in postproduction.

IT NEVER RAINS, BUT IT POURS!

Buckbeak was placed in the Scottish hillside location by means of a crane, "which was a ghastly experience," creature effects supervisor Nick Dudman recalls. "This was done during the middle of a soaking rainstorm. The muddy hillside's being washed off, then replaced with more mud, and it's all rolling down!" Nick was concerned about rain getting into the creature's electronics. "It's not something you can service easily," he continues. "You can't run off to the nearest shop and buy a new part! And while filming, we had to stop every two minutes because of downpours of rain or hail and throw tarpaulins over it to protect it, while all the time we're sliding about in the mud. It certainly wasn't the way to treat a complex animatronic creature!" But Nick admits, "We got some great footage, so, you know, in the end, it was all worth it."

Biting Hot

"You're not dangerous
at all, are you, you
great ugly brute."

—Draco Malfoy, *Harry Potter and the Prisoner of Azkaban*

Actor Tom Felton, who played Draco Malfoy, remembers his scenes with Buckbeak, which were shot in Black Park, about an hour west of London. "I remember it very clearly," he says with a laugh, "because it was very sunny and very hot that day. We did the first shots with our black robes on over our clothes, but that changed immediately! It was so bloody hot, you'll notice that all the top buttons on our shirts are undone." Many of the students were also allowed to take their robes off. Draco fails to follow Hagrid's advice and storms up to Buckbeak without the proper etiquette, only to get struck down. "Hagrid picks me up, but in order for that to work size-wise, they had to make a very realistic one-third size life cast of me," Tom says. "I asked if I could take it home. I thought it was a brilliant thing; I could have put it in my bed, like I was sleeping, and go out!"

Make It Your Own

One of the great things about IncrediBuilds models is that each one is completely customizable. The untreated natural wood can be decorated with paints, pencils, pens, beads, sequins—the list goes on and on!

When making a replica, it's always good to study an actual image of what you are trying to copy. Look closely at the images in this book and brainstorm how you can re-create them.

Before you start building and decorating your model, though, read through the included instruction sheet so you understand how all the pieces come together. Then, choose a theme and make a plan. Do you want to make an exact replica of Buckbeak or something completely different? The choice is yours! Here is an example to get those creative juices flowing.

WHAT YOU NEED

- Black, white, gray, golden yellow, and red paint
- Paintbrush

WHAT YOU MIGHT WANT

- Gouache (used in example)

GOUACHE PAINT is a type of opaque watercolor that blends very nicely. You can find it at your local arts and crafts store. If you don't have gouache, acrylic paint will work, too.

PAINTING BUCKBEAK

1. Assemble the model, but leave the wings off.

2. Start by painting the midsection of the model white. This includes Buckbeak's front legs, chest, and stomach.

3. Paint Buckbeak's back legs, tail, and head gray.

4. Add an extra coat of gray to the beak.

5. Paint the ends of the front legs gray.

6. Since Buckbeak's feathers are speckled, go over the white midsection with small dabs of gray paint. Blend them in with the white background until you achieve the effect you like.

7. Now, go over the gray back legs, tail, and head with white paint. Add small dabs of paint, and blend them in until you are happy with the effect.

8. Finish with the small details: white hooves, black claws, and golden eyes.

PAINTING THE WINGS

1. On the engraved side, paint the top section of feathers white. Speckle them with gray just as you did on Buckbeak's body.

2. Paint the rest of the feathers gray.

3. Using a small paintbrush, carefully paint stripes onto each feather with a lighter shade of gray.

4. For the unengraved side of the wings, paint the top of each wing white.

5. Paint the rest of the wing gray, and add speckles of white over it.

6. Finish by adding a section of vertical black markings down the middle of the wings where the white meets the gray.

IncrediBuilds™
A Division of Insight Editions, LP
PO Box 3088
San Rafael, CA 94912
www.insighteditions.com

 Find us on Facebook: www.facebook.com/InsightEditions

Follow us on Twitter: @insighteditions

Library of Congress Cataloging-in-Publication Data available.

ISBN: 978-1-68298-157-3

Publisher: Raoul Goff
Associate Publisher: Vanessa Lopez
Art Director: Chrissy Kwasnik
Designers: Jenelle Wagner and Ashley Quackenbush
Managing Editor: Molly Glover
Project Editor: Greg Solano
Production Editors: Elaine Ou and Carly Chillmon
Editorial Assistants: Warren Buchanan and Hilary VandenBroek
Associate Production Manager: Sam Taylor
Model Designer: Ryan Zhang, Team Green

Buckbeak visual development artwork by Dermot Power, Paul Catling, and Andrew Williamson.

INSIGHT EDITIONS would like to thank Victoria Selover, Melanie Swartz, Elaine Piechowski, Ashley Bol, Margo Guffin, George Valdiviez, and Kevin Morris.

 REPLANTED PAPER

Insight Editions, in association with Roots of Peace, will plant two trees for each tree used in the manufacturing of this book. Roots of Peace is an internationally renowned humanitarian organization dedicated to eradicating land mines worldwide and converting war-torn lands into productive farms and wildlife habitats. Roots of Peace will plant two million fruit and nut trees in Afghanistan and provide farmers there with the skills and support necessary for sustainable land use.

Manufactured in Shaoguan, China, by Insight Editions

10 9 8 7 6 5 4 3 2 1